THIS CANDLEWICK BOOK BELONGS TO:

_____

_____

_____

For Kelli Huffman, a true friend; and in memory of her Nana,
Libbye G. Prawde

First paperback edition 2017

Library of Congress Cataloging-in-Publication Data is available.

Library of Congress Catalog Card Number 2007940978

ISBN 978-0-7636-3614-2 (hardcover)
ISBN 978-0-7636-9312-1 (paperback)

20 21 22 APS 10 9 8 7 6 5 4 3

Printed in Humen, Dongguan, China

This book was typeset in Triplex Serif Light.
The illustrations were done in ink and acrylic, combined digitally.

Candlewick Press
99 Dover Street
Somerville, Massachusetts 02144

visit us at www.candlewick.com

CECE BELL

BEE-WIGGED

Three cheers
for Jerry!

CANDLEWICK PRESS

Jerry Bee loved people.

But people did not love Jerry Bee.

For one thing, he was a bee.

For another, he was the most enormous bee anyone had ever seen.

A sting from a bee Jerry's size would really hurt.

So people stayed away.

It's true that Jerry was quite large. But he had never stung anyone in his entire life.

In fact, he had tried hard to make friends.

But nothing worked.

One morning, Jerry saw an old wig lying on the sidewalk. *Why not?* thought Jerry. And he put the wig on his head.

Just then, he heard a bus driver shout, "Young man, you're late for school!" The bus driver stopped her bus, opened the door, and hollered, "Get in!"

Jerry got on the bus.

As Jerry looked at himself in the mirror, he had a wonderful thought: If he looked like a boy instead of a bee, maybe people would finally like him!

When the bus stopped, Jerry made a beeline for the school. He couldn't wait to make friends with all the people inside!

Jerry entered the first classroom he could find.

"Excuse me, ma'am," he said. "My name is Jerry, and I would love to join your wonderful class. And might I add that you are looking quite lovely today?"

Miss Swann was the first friend Jerry made that day.

The students really liked
Jerry, too.

He was helpful,

funny,

artistic,

and generous.

He was even a terrific speller.

By the end of the day, Jerry Bee had more friends
than he had ever had in his life.

So Jerry decided to come to school every day.
And every day, he made more friends.

One day, he helped the janitor mop.

The next day, he complimented the lunch ladies on their food.

Jerry inspired the cheerleaders with his remarkable team spirit.

He even won over the bus driver.

By the end of the week, everyone loved Jerry so much . . .

that they made him the grand marshal of the annual school parade!

Jerry Bee was ecstatic. He couldn't believe how much the wig had changed his life.

Then the wind started blowing. Hard.

The wind blew Jerry's wig right off his head!

He tried to catch it, but . . .

he was too late.

Everyone saw Jerry without the wig, and everyone saw that he was the most enormous bee they had ever seen.

"Wait!" shouted a voice.

It was the wig!

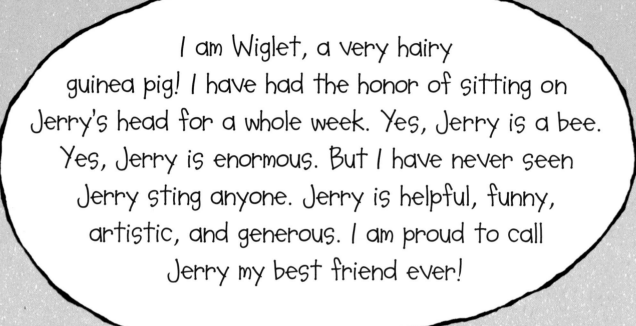

I am Wiglet, a very hairy guinea pig! I have had the honor of sitting on Jerry's head for a whole week. Yes, Jerry is a bee. Yes, Jerry is enormous. But I have never seen Jerry sting anyone. Jerry is helpful, funny, artistic, and generous. I am proud to call Jerry my best friend ever!

Everyone was quiet. And then . . .

"HOORAY for Jerry Bee! HOORAY

for Wiglet! HIP, HIP, HOORAY!"

everyone shouted.

It was the best day of Jerry Bee's life.
At last he could be himself *and* have friends.

And Wiglet would be his best friend forever.

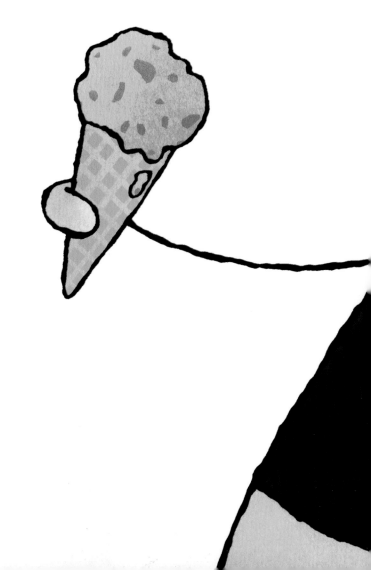

Author's Note

Bee-Wigged is my favorite book of all the books I've done. It's also an autobiography—a fact that I didn't even realize until I held the book in my hands for the first time.

Jerry Bee's story is my story. Of course, I wasn't a giant bee who wore a wig in order to look like a boy. But I was a kid who felt different from all the other kids, and I wore a big clunky hearing aid in order to hear more like they could. Like Jerry, I wanted very much to have friends. Like Jerry, I tried to be helpful, funny, artistic, and generous—and to be really good at spelling.

Jerry's great fear was that his classmates would find out just how different he was, and that when they did, they would no longer wish to be his friend. I had the exact same fear. But thankfully, Jerry's wig turns out to be the very hairy guinea pig Wiglet, who reminds everyone just how great Jerry is—and my hearing aid turned out to be something that my classmates really dug once they saw all the fun things that I could do with it.

Bee-Wigged is a story about accepting people—and bees—who might be different from you. It's also a reminder that being helpful, funny, artistic, and generous can go a long way in one's quest for friends. (But don't worry if you aren't good at spelling. That doesn't matter, except when you forget the *r* in *friends*—try not to call your friends your fiends!)

Cece Bell is the author-illustrator of many children's books, including the Theodor Seuss Geisel Honor Book *Rabbit and Robot: The Sleepover* and the Newbery Honor–winning graphic novel *El Deafo*. Cece Bell lives in Virginia with her husband, author Tom Angleberger.